ANYTHING CAN HAPPEN,
YOU JUST HAVE TO BELIEVE!

Minerva
Mint

STONE ARCH BOOKS
a capstone imprint

Minerva Mint is first published in the United States in 2015 by Stone Arch Books
A Capstone Imprint
1710 Roe Crest Drive
North Mankato, Minnesota 56003
www.capstonepub.com

Editorial project by Atlantyca Dreamfarm S.r.l.

Text by Elisa Puricelli Guerra
Illustrations by Gabo Leon Bernstein
Translation by Marco Zeni
Original edition published by Edizioni Piemme S.p.A., Italy
Original title: La foresta degli alberi parlanti

International Rights © Atlantyca S.p.A., via Leopardi 8 – 20123 Milano – Italia —
foreignrights@atlantyca.it — www.atlantyca.com

Library of Congress Cataloging-in-Publication Data is available
on the Library of Congress website.

ISBN: 978-1-62370-181-9 (hardcover)
ISBN: 978-1-4342-9673-3 (library binding)
ISBN: 978-1-4342-9676-4 (paperback)
ISBN: 978-1-4965-0193-6 (eBook)

Summary:
The Order of the Owls answers a call for help by traveling to a supposedly enchanted forest.

Designer:
Rick Korab

Printed in China.
032015   008866RRDF15

THE FOREST
OF
TALKING TREES

by Elisa Puricelli Guerra

illustrated by Gabo León Bernstein

TABLE OF CONTENTS

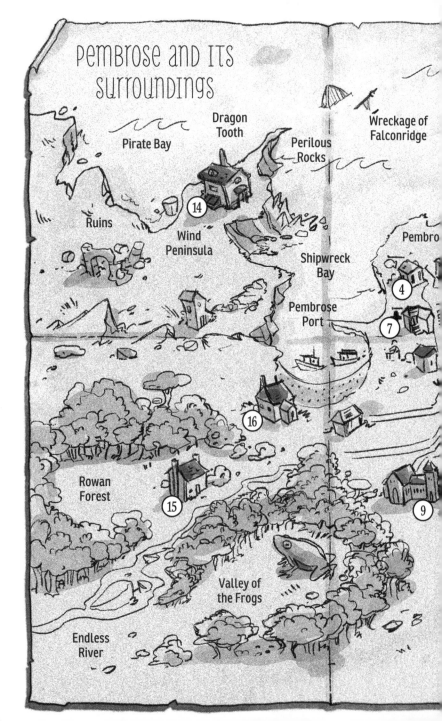

Turtle Island

Admiral Rock

Giant Rock

Seagull Peninsula

Traitor Rock

Circle of Stones

Owl Tower

Valley of Heather

Rainbow Fish Lake

Bodmin Heath Moor

Knight Hill

Alder Swamp

Agatha's Cottage

Lizard Manor
Crowley Hall
Smuggler's Den
Fishbone Inn
Post Office
Bon Ton Clothing Shop
Dr. Gerald's Clinic
Church

9. School
10. Gilbert O'Sullivan's House
11. Owl Tower
12. Agatha's Cottage
13. Tintagel Castle
14. The Lone Pirate Inn
15. Old House of Sighs
16. Fisherman Circle

WHAT'S HAPPENED SO FAR...

Minerva Mint is a nine-year-old girl living in Lizard Manor atop Admiral Rock in Cornwall, England. She lives with fourteen snowy owls, six foxes, and a badger named Hugo. She also shares the house with Geraldine Flopps, the kind custodian who found Minerva in a suitcase at Victoria station when the girl was just a few months old.

Minerva is determined to find out what happened to her parents, but it's no easy task. Very few hints were left in the bag: a volume from the Universal Encyclopedia, *an envelope addressed to someone named Septimus Hodge, and the deed to the Cornwall mansion. She has tried to solve the mystery by herself for several years, but now she finally has help: her new friends Ravi and Thomasina.*

With them, she has found out that she descends from a pirate and a beautiful witch named Althea. They were both members of a gang of rogues, the Ravagers of the Sea, who wreaked havoc on the Cornish coasts three centuries before. Betrayed by their evil leader Black Bart, Althea managed to steal and stash away the riches the Ravagers had collected shortly before she died. She left the one and only clue to the treasure's location with her newborn baby, along with a powerful amulet: a small flute that can call hundreds of owls. Minerva and her friends found the flute in Lizard Manor inside a little box hidden in the wall.

What happened to Althea's daughter, though? And what happened to the greatest treasure that has ever existed?

CHAPTER 1

HERE COME THE WATERMELONS!

A new, sunny summer day had just begun in the quiet village of Pembrose. The sun glittered in the water, barely ruffled by a light breeze. A few rowboats bobbed up and down off the coast, though the fishermen seemed much more interested in getting a nap than casting their lines. The cobblestone alleys that snaked up from the harbor to the village were cool and shaded, and the tiny front yards of the houses were adorned by roses and lilacs. (In one short week, the local horticultural club would announce the winner of the Green Thumb Cup, and the villagers had suddenly discovered a burning passion for gardening.)

Delicious scents of eggs, bacon, and toast were coming from the open windows. It was time to eat breakfast and read the local newspaper, where the people of Pembrose could find the news they would later gossip about in the main square.

Gwendolyn Bartholomew had gotten up earlier than usual. She had paid extra care in choosing her clothes and had started to sweep the doorstep of the shop she owned with her sister. When she heard a noise, she straightened up and smiled: Timothy Long had just come out to pick up the newspaper that was lying in front of his restaurant's main door. "Good day!" She smiled at him, glowing.

The man startled and lowered his gaze upon his brownish cardigan, which was quite worn and covered in tomato sauce stains. That morning, he had decided to try out a new recipe for stewed mussels. "Ah, Gwendolyn," he said, covering the largest stain with the newspaper. "B-beautiful day," he stammered.

"I . . . I mean . . ." He then realized that he was still wearing his slippers and fell silent with embarrassment. He would have felt even more unease if he had known that someone was spying on them.

"*Ugh!* Nothing interesting ever happens in this village!" Thomasina moaned. "Just Gwendolyn making sheep's eyes at Timothy. *Boooring!*"

"Come on, you can't say that nothing happens in Pembrose!" Ravi whispered to her.

"Well, nothing's happening *now*," the girl replied.

Ravi decided that Thomasina was the only person who would wish for a new adventure before even eating breakfast. As far as he was concerned, all he wanted was some toast with jam. But he had to stay where he was: sitting watch.

The two of them were hidden behind a bunch of bushel baskets full of watermelons, ready to be loaded on Bert's little van. Bert sold fruits and vegetables in the neighboring villages.

Minerva was hiding behind a short wall across the street. You could only see a couple of red curls and her green, lively eyes popping up every now and then.

"I've had enough of this funeral!" Thomasina blurted out. "We're supposed to be spies on an important mission!"

Ravi looked at the notepad Thomasina was holding in her lap. She hadn't written down one single significant event. "Maybe we should go spy somewhere else," he suggested. "Somewhere where more important things happen."

"Good idea," Thomasina said, waving at Minerva.

The girl responded by gesturing toward the harbor.

"Okay, let's move," Thomasina whispered to Ravi. "Just make sure you don't give us away."

Hurt, Ravi shrugged his shoulders: why did Thomasina always have to talk to him as if he were a little child?

A second later, he lost his balance. He had been crouching for so long that the moment he stood up his legs gave out on him. He instinctively leaned on the basket in front of him, tipping it over and making it hit the one standing next to it. That set off a terrible domino effect. Watermelons started to roll down the steep alley, just as a group of tourists started to work their way up the road on the other side. The out-of-towners, however, were too busy taking pictures of the little cottages to realize what was happening.

"Oh no!" Minerva exclaimed as she hopped over the wall and darted after the watermelons, waving her arms frantically. "Watch out! Get out of the way!"

Pulled out of his embarrassment, the innkeeper behaved like a real knight. He swept Gwendolyn up in his arms, rescuing her from the danger.

"Timothy . . ." She sighed with her arms around his neck.

"Watch out! Here come the watermelons! Run for cover!" Minerva shouted again, running past them. "Make *waaay!* Make *waaay!*"

Her warnings were pointless. The tourists were facing the other way, gazing at a small church. They were all wearing earphones and listening

to a recording of the village's history.

Luckily, Minerva Mint was a fierce runner and had almost caught up with the melons. "Here come the watermelons!"

Thomasina and Ravi tried to keep up with her. The girl's blond curls flew up with charm, and her cheeks turned a rosy pink, making her even more beautiful. At least, that's what Ravi thought as he sneaked a peek at her.

"Why are you always doing these things?" Thomasina complained, shattering the magic of the moment.

"You were just saying that nothing ever happens around here . . ." replied a hurt Ravi.

"Look *ouuut!* WATERMELONS AHOY!" Minerva screamed at the top of her lungs.

At long last, the tourists turned around, and then the trouble really began.

Luckily, though, Minerva was also an ace at solving difficult situations.

* * *

"Ah, I'm feeling so much better!" Ravi said with a sigh a couple of hours later, rolling onto his stomach on the grass.

Nothing was better than a picnic of warm scones and Mrs. Flopps's strawberry jam to forget a disastrous morning.

Ravi, Minerva, and Thomasina were lying in the front yard of Lizard Manor, at the top of Admiral Rock, a place that overlooked both the village and the ocean. Fourteen snowy owls were flying back and forth from the mansion's roof, as if they had been interested in listening to their conversation or, more likely, lured by the leftovers.

"Just a little later, and I would have starved to death," the boy added.

"Oh, please, Ravi!" Thomasina snorted, using a handkerchief to wipe jam off her sticky hands. Then she turned to Minerva, who was still chewing on her scone. "Those tourists were really rude! They didn't even thank us for saving their lives."

"Well, we didn't *technically* save their lives . . ." Ravi said. "And to be honest, it was our fault."

"*Your* fault you mean!" Thomasina said.

Minerva gobbled up her scone and stepped in to put an end to what must have been their umpteenth fight. "What matters is that it all ended well," she told her friends.

Indeed, alerted by her yelling, the tourists had managed to find shelter behind a lush rhododendron bush, and the watermelons weren't even damaged in the fall. Putting them all back into the bushels, however, had been a real struggle.

"We're going to have to work as gardeners now, though." Ravi sighed.

Unfortunately for them, the largest watermelon had rolled straight into the front yard of Orazia Haddok, the village's feared nurse, crushing her beloved hyacinths. Minerva, Ravi, and Thomasina had spent the rest of the morning planting new plants, and to get her forgiveness, they had promised to take care of the new plants on a daily basis.

"Gardening is one of the most boring things in the world!" Thomasina moaned. "We're going to waste time that should be spent looking for the Dragon!"

In the last few days, the three friends had been keeping a close eye on the people of Pembrose. They were determined to find the author of two messages sent to the Order of the Owls — messages that were signed *The Dragon*. That's how they had wound up in the sticky situation a couple of hours earlier.

"We haven't learned one single detail about his identity," Thomasina complained. "He, however, knows everything about us . . . including the fact that we're looking for the Ravagers' treasure." She snorted. "I'm sure he's waiting for us to find it so he can get his own hands on it!"

"Why wouldn't he just look for it on his own?" asked Ravi, eyeing a bit of scone that had eluded him.

"Maybe he tried . . . but couldn't find it," Thomasina replied. "We're not going to let him take it away from us, are we, Minerva?"

"Of course not!" her friend confirmed. And the light burning in her eyes spoke the exact same truth.

"How are we going to defend ourselves from him when we don't even know who he is?" Ravi pointed out as a chill ran down his spine. On that warm and shiny day, the Dragon seemed to him like a black cloud full of rain and lightning.

The three friends shot each other a discouraged look. On the surface, Pembrose looked like a sleepy fishermen village, but its people were a proud and independent lot, rugged like the cliffs shaped by the wind and the sea. Their ancestors were bootleggers, pirates, raiders, and rogues of all sorts. Therefore, it was quite possible that the Dragon could be hiding among their descendants and that he was a very dangerous person.

"He could even be someone we know . . ." said Thomasina in a whisper.

Minerva stood up. "You know what? Since we're going to be busy taking care of Mrs. Haddok's garden tomorrow, we should make the best of the rest of today." A sly grin appeared on her freckled, little face. "I've got an idea . . ."

"Hooray!" Thomasina sprung to her feet and straightened her delicate cotton dress that made her look like a butterfly. "What are we going to do?"

Ravi felt a sharp pang in his stomach: the most logical explanation was that he had eaten too many scones. However, since his arrival in Pembrose, he had began to believe in signs and omens, and a stomachache could be a clear warning sign.

We started off the day on the wrong foot, he said to himself as he followed his friends home, *and bad is the only way it's going to end . . . bad for me.*

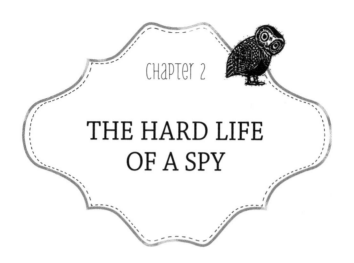

CHapter 2

THE HARD LIFE
OF A SPY

Lizard Manor's front door was hidden behind a huge
pile of baskets filled with jars of homemade jam.
Mrs. Flopps was about to leave for Truro, where she
took part in the local fair once a month. Mrs. Flopps's
business thrived in August, thanks to the tourists.
Bert was going to drop by any time now to pick her
up and give her a ride in his van.

Minerva led Ravi and Thomasina through the
house's dark entrance hall.

"What's on your mind?" Thomasina whispered,
champing at the bit to know her friend's plans.

"Follow me . . . and you'll find out," she replied, giving them each a candle.

Ravi would have loved to go back to the sun-flooded garden, but he stuck by his friends. As the girls talked to one another, Ravi tried to dodge the cobwebs hanging from the ceiling. All of a sudden, he felt something scurrying down his neck and began to wriggle like an eel to get it off.

"Hey!" Thomasina said. "You hit me with your elbow!"

Ravi, however, didn't even hear his friend's complaint, because he had caught a glimpse of a terrifying shape coming out of the darkness. Were his worst fears finally coming true? Had one of Lizard Manor's ghosts decided to show itself at last?

In fact, it was just Mrs. Flopps holding a fox in her arms.

"Ginger injured his foot," she said. "I'm taking him to Truro with me so the vet can look at him."

Lizard Manor's living room number three was home to six foxes. Like Minerva, Geraldine Flopps loved animals and would never turn away a living creature seeking shelter or medical attention.

"Have a nice trip, Mrs. Flopps!" the three children said in unison.

"I'll be back on Monday," said the woman. "The fridge is full, and there's a basket of scones, fresh out of the oven, on the table."

The woman adjusted her elegant hat, which she wore only when she went to town, and, whistling a

popular sailor song, walked out the front door with a wave.

The three children waved back and then went up the stairs under the watchful eye of Minerva's ancestors, who grimly stared at them from the portraits hanging on the walls. The most threatening was definitely Merrival M., the terrible Ravager of the Seas.

"The dust must have settled in town by now," Minerva said, leading her friends up to the third floor. "To be sure, however, I thought we could disguise ourselves!" she said, entering one of the manor's thirty-one bedrooms. "If the tourists are still in Pembrose, they won't recognize us if we are in disguise." She threw open the doors of a wardrobe. "There are some very interesting clothes in here . . ."

Minerva never bought clothes. She found all she needed in Lizard Manor's chests and wardrobes.

"Great idea!" Thomasina agreed. "I don't want to have to take care of yet another garden . . ." she added, giving Ravi a rude look.

The boy ignored her; he had figured out that it

was the most successful tactic whenever Thomasina picked on him. He started to study the clothes.

Minerva chose an outfit that could be best described as a female version of Sherlock Holmes, with a pretty pleated skirt and a tweed cap.

Ravi dressed as a fisherman, including rubber boots and a hat pulled down over his eyes.

Thomasina chose a shiny silk dress, complete with a huge ribbon on the front. The icing on the cake was a little hat that had made her sigh the very moment she had spotted it in the back. It was adorned with feathers and had a pink chinstrap.

"How do I look?" she asked, twirling. "Well? What's the matter?" she pressed, aware of Ravi's puzzled look.

"Nothing," he was quick to answer. "You look just great. However . . . don't you think you're a little too flashy?" he dared add. "To be a spy, I mean . . ."

"I'm more natural when I'm wearing elegant clothes," Thomasina replied firmly.

Ravi made no further comments. He realized that

people would recognize them in spite of their disguises, but dressing up was just too much fun!

It turned out that riding her bike in the silk skirt was no piece of cake, but Thomasina didn't let it show. So they all sailed along the cliff, keeping away from the area controlled by that awful Gilbert and his vicious dog, William the Conqueror: they had already had enough trouble for the day.

Their bike baskets held notepads, binoculars, and

the handheld mirrors they used to communicate long distance with Morse code.

When they arrived in Pembrose, they once again started spying on unsuspecting citizens. They set up post in different spots around the village, but once more, nothing interesting happened. Everybody seemed to be intent on watering their little gardens, dreaming of the first prize.

"Being a spy is the world's most boring job,"

Thomasina said with a yawn when they met to discuss what each one had seen.

"What have we found out so far?" Minerva asked.

Ravi looked at his notepad. "Not much," he replied. "Timothy almost poisoned a customer at lunch. Pembrose Knitting Club is about to be closed because Mrs. Trout cheated at Petit Point. The Bartholomew Sisters are cultivating a special kind of rose that they haven't shown anybody, with the hopes of winning the Green Thumb Cup."

Thomasina yawned again. "You know what? I'm tired of being a spy!" she blurted. "There's not enough action."

"I think we've had some action today!" Ravi replied. "And all thanks to me," he couldn't help adding. However, he immediately realized he had said the wrong thing.

"Hush!" Minerva said.

They were now in a sheltered spot next to Dr. Gerald's office. Agatha Willow was coming their way, a basket hanging on her arm.

"She's bringing her homemade cough syrups to the doctor," whispered Ravi.

Agatha was their friend. She lived all alone in a cottage out in Bodmin Heath Moor. She had a reputation for being a witch among the people of Pembrose, though she always said that the only potions she prepared were her syrups made from wild plants.

In that moment there was a thunderous sneeze. *"ACHOOO!"*

"Bless you!" Minerva said immediately.

"That wasn't me," Ravi said.

"That wasn't me either," Thomasina added.

"TCHEE-OO!" A second sneeze echoed loud and clear. It sounded like it was coming from above.

Three noses rose up, and the children saw a bird circling over their heads, its feathers as black as coal.

"Was that you?" asked Minerva, shading her eyes with her hand.

"TCHEE-OO!" answered the bird, gliding down toward them. Its feet and beak were bright red.

Minerva glanced about. "Could you please go a bit

further on?" she asked politely. "You're going to give us away!" The little bird, however, kept making its funny sound.

"He's making fun of us!" Ravi grunted, waving his hands to shoo it away. "The last thing we need is for him to get the whole village's attention!"

The black bird flew in a wide circle, then landed near them on the edge of the river, which at that point — a few feet from the harbor — was little more than a stream. *"TCHEE-OO!"* it repeated louder than ever.

"Hush!" said Ravi. "Can't you see we're on a secret mission?"

The bird's little, shiny eyes glittered lively and sharply. Minerva grew curious about him. "*Mmm*, I think he's trying to tell us something."

"In my opinion, he's just a pain in the neck!" Ravi blurted, pulling his hat over his eyes, certain that someone was going to show up any minute.

"Maybe he's hungry," Thomasina suggested. She opened her purse, fished out a pastry made by Crowley Hall's chef, and gave it to the bird.

"Hey!" Ravi protested. "That's our snack!"

"Just *your* share," Thomasina replied and hunkered down toward the little bird, holding the pastry.

The bird, however, shook its head and started pecking at something that was sticking out of the ground. More and more curious, Minerva stepped closer to take a look.

The little bird stepped aside, and she started digging. "There's something here . . ."

The neck of a closed bottle surfaced before the bewildered eyes of the three friends. It had a cork stopper and was encrusted with dirt, little stones, and seashells. The red-curled girl grabbed it with both hands and yanked it out of the ground.

They studied it with great curiosity, but the glass was too dirty for them to see if there was anything inside. Minerva started cleaning it. "I wonder where it came from . . ."

"Maybe someone threw it in the river," Thomasina guessed. "The current might have carried it over here, where it got stuck."

"TCHEE-OO!" their winged friend said.

Agatha, who had just walked out of the doctor's office, heard the sound and rushed over to the three kids. "Hi!" she yelled, walking toward them.

At that point, the little bird unfolded its black wings and soared, heading toward the ocean.

Surprised, Agatha raised her head and followed its flight with her sky-blue eyes. "What are you doing here?" she muttered under her breath, frowning.

"Look what we found!" Minerva said, holding up the bottle.

Agatha turned toward her young friend for a moment, and when she turned to face the ocean again, she could barely see as the black bird's tail disappeared round Cape Pembrose.

Still puzzled, she walked up to the kids. "What's with the clothes?" she asked, unable to stifle a smile.

"Oh, we're rehearsing for a Halloween party," Ravi mumbled.

As usual, the lie gave Minerva an unpleasant tickling feeling between her toes. She ignored it, however, because she had made an incredible discovery. "Hey, there's something inside the bottle!" she exclaimed. A scroll could be seen through the glass.

"I can't believe it," Thomasina cheered. "We've found a message! Come on, open it!"

Minerva removed the stopper. "Are you ready?" she asked her friends before pulling out the scroll.

Ravi nodded and felt a terrible pang in his stomach. Were his feelings about to be confirmed?

CHAPTER 3

A REQUEST
FOR HELP

Minerva took the scroll out of the bottle and held it in the palm of her outstretched hand, savoring that magical moment when the future holds the promise of an adventure.

When she finally unrolled the scroll, all four of them were amazed.

"It's not paper," Thomasina said. "It looks like leaves sewn together."

And that was exactly what it was: six large, oblong leaves that had been sewn together with thin brown thread.

A message was written on the scroll: *My parents are gone, and I really need help. I don't know if I'll be able to make it on my own. If you find this message, come look for me in Rowan Forest. Please, come quick. Morgana.*

As they skimmed through the message, the three friends leaned over until their heads touched. Agatha leaned over to take a look too, and her mouth became taut with worry.

"A request for help!" Minerva exclaimed.

"It looks like a little girl wrote this . . ." Thomasina guessed.

"But where is Rowan Forest?" asked a puzzled Ravi.

"It's up the hill along the river," replied Agatha. Her forehead was wrinkled and her voice was serious. "That forest is no place for kids."

Minerva looked at her, surprised. "We *have* to go there to look for Morgana," she replied.

The young woman shook her head. "That bottle has probably been buried for several years." She pointed at the dirt encrusted on the glass. "It's too late now."

Minerva clenched her fists stubbornly. "How can you be so sure?"

Agatha picked up the scroll. "The leaves tell me," she replied. "They are very old."

Minerva shot to her feet, her red curls dancing like little flames. "It's never too late to answer someone's call for help!" she said firmly. She looked over at her friends. "Am I right, guys?"

"Right!" Thomasina echoed her.

Ravi studied the bottle, uncertain of what to do. "Why did you say that Rowan Forest is no place for kids?" he asked Agatha.

Their friend knew a whole lot about that part of Cornwall. She knew the secrets and the legends that the Pembrose gossips barely had the courage to tell each other in whispers.

"It's one of Great Britain's oldest surviving forests," Agatha replied. "It's more than one thousand years old. Many have tried to explore it, never to return. There are no trails; the forest rubs them out every time someone tries to make them," she explained. "And that's not all, tricky paths also appear, leading the travelers astray. It's like the forest doesn't like strangers, so much so that the people from neighboring villages have stopped trying to venture into it."

Ravi looked at his friends. Agatha's words gave him the creeps, but Minerva and Thomasina didn't look worried at all. It was typical of them: the scarier the place, the more they wanted to go there!

"There's one more thing that might make you think twice about the idea of venturing there," Agatha added. "There's an ancient legend about Rowan Forest . . . and you know that old legends always have a little bit of truth, don't you?"

The three friends knew that very well: they had gotten into trouble every time they had decided to challenge Cornwall's ancient legends. Like the time when they had explored the magical cave under Tintagel's castle, or when they had faced the Terror of the Seas, or the time when Black Bart's ghost scared everyone in town but them.

"The trees that make up the forest are believed to be the people from the villages that opposed King Arthur's rule," Agatha continued. "Arthur was unifying Cornwall into one kingdom and asked the villagers to give up. When the people revolted, they were turned into trees by Merlin, the powerful sorcerer and the king's right-hand man." Her voice lowered to a whisper. "Every single person in the villages became a tree: men, women, and children."

Ravi was shocked. "But . . . wasn't Arthur a good king?" Everyone in Cornwall knew about the deeds of Arthur and his Knights of the Round Table. The famous king had been born and had lived near Pembrose.

"Arthur was a brave warrior, and he became a wise king," replied Agatha. "But he believed he had to create a unified kingdom so that he could better defend the land from the threat of foreign attacks. Therefore, every county and every village had to give up their freedom and fall under his rule. Cornwall, however, has always been a proud and wild land, filled with people who bravely wanted their independence and were ready to fight for it. Like the people from the village of Honey Combe and their neighbors, who were punished for standing up for their rights."

"By being turned into trees?" butted in Ravi, unbelieving.

Agatha nodded sadly. "They have kept their plant form for a thousand years." She sighed. "But that's not all . . ."

Minerva was listening closely to every word. Unlike Ravi, she was dying to go to the forest. She could feel her legs prickle with the desire to move, as if she had been hit by some kind of itchy allergy.

"You see, trees are mysterious creatures," Agatha continued. "Their life does not depend on humans and, unlike us, they ponder every decision they make. When they do make up their mind, however . . . no one can stop them." A gust of wind whipped up her long black hair, sending wild waves raging around her face. "One day, according to the legend, when they face another injustice, the trees will awaken and fight back. Then we're all going to be in deep trouble. That is why you mustn't go into the forest, especially not alone."

To Ravi's great surprise, Minerva glanced at Thomasina and nodded, as if she had given up.

Agatha drew a sigh of relief. "Nobody really knows trees," she explained in a somewhat more relaxed tone. "They are extraordinary creatures. They live for hundreds of years and hold humankind's every secret. They have heard all of the stories told around campfires: stories of loves, friendships, and betrayals . . ."

Just then, the clock of the village's little church struck five. The young woman shook out of her thoughts. "I have to go," she said. "I'm running late with my deliveries." She gave the scroll back to Minerva and added, "I'm sorry, we really can't do anything to help Morgana." Her voice grew softer. "I know it's hard to accept that."

She picked up the basket that she had laid on the ground and, making for Plum Avenue, waved good-bye. "So long, come see me in the heath moor soon. I'll bake one of my special cakes for you!"

At the sound of those words, Ravi put a hand on his stomach. "How about some sna—" he started to say once Agatha was far enough, but the fighting light that sparkled in his friends' eyes suddenly made him lose his appetite.

"We've got to find a way to cross the forest," Minerva decided, looking at Thomasina.

Ravi was shocked. "I thought you didn't want to go . . ."

The girl shrugged. "Oh, no," she replied. "I just wanted to get rid of Agatha."

"Good move!" Thomasina said.

"But you heard what she said," Ravi insisted. "All those who went into the forest never came back."

Minerva smiled. "Well, we will." She stepped closer to her friend and looked him straight in the eye. "Ravi Kapoor, a member of the Order of the Owls never backs down when someone needs help. You should know that by now!"

Thomasina put her face close to the boy's and tried to soften him with one of her stunning smiles. "Come on, Ravi. We have to find out if Morgana is okay. I'm sure you want to know too."

He stood firm, determined to say no.

Minerva took him by the arm. "How about we have a little snack while we think about it, huh?"

Ravi loosened up a little. That was one offer he could not refuse.

The kids bought three traditional Cornish meat and onion pasties and went to sit on the wharf. They were so absorbed by their conversation that they didn't notice the way the villagers kept looking at their odd outfits.

"How are we even going to get to the forest?" mumbled Ravi with his mouth full. The excellent pasty had brightened up his spirits. "Did you hear what she said? There are no trails."

"That's right," Minerva said. "And it's too far to walk it." She had taken off her shoes and dipped her feet in the cool water to clear her thoughts. "We surely can't bike through the forest either . . ." She turned to look at the river behind their back and her face lit up. "Mmm, maybe there is a way . . ." She put her shoes back on and picked up the bottle, which she had sat on the wharf boards. "Follow me!" she ordered.

Thomasina threw the last morsels of pasty to the fish and shook her magnificent dress. "Where are we going?"

Minerva pointed at an older man who was sitting on the pier and enjoying the sun in the company of a small group of lobster fishermen. He was Jim, a retired sailor who liked to spend his time fishing on the river.

"I've got it!" Thomasina exclaimed. "You want to use his raft!"

The man was very proud of the raft he had made with his own hands and had shown it to everybody in Pembrose.

"That's right," Minerva confirmed. "The river is too shallow in spots for our boat, but Jim keeps his raft anchored out of the village, where the water's deeper."

Ravi followed his friend with a sigh. "How can you be so sure that he'll agree to give us his raft?"

"I can be very convincing," Minerva replied, winking at him. "Anyway, this is the ideal time to go: Mrs. Flopps is in Truro, and Thomasina's parents are going to be salmon fishing in Scotland until Monday. You can tell your mother that you're going to spend the weekend at my place. Tomorrow's Friday . . ." She paused, thinking. "If we leave at dawn, I'm sure we'll be back by Monday."

Ravi made one last try. "What about Mrs. Haddok's garden?" he asked. "You know she's expecting us tomorrow, don't you?"

Minerva thought about it. "Well," she replied with a wide grin, "she'll just have to wait a little longer!"

CHAPTER 4

WHO'S AFRAID OF THE BIG BAD WOLF?

That night, a small black bird with a red beak circled over the village of Pembrose, which slept like a kitten curled up into a ball between the cliffs. The villagers were snoring away in their comfortable beds, unaware of the wrongs done to their neighbors centuries before. As far as they knew, they had nothing to fear in their little village; they didn't even have to lock their doors.

The clock in the bell tower struck four, as wings blacker than the night itself grazed the church roof, hiding the thin slice of moon for a moment. As soon as the newcomer reached Admiral Rock, fourteen snowy owls, perched on the roof, stared suspiciously at it with their round yellow eyes. But the snowy owls were not the only ones who were awake: a light came on behind a window on the third floor.

A second light responded from the Pembrose post office, and a third one came on behind the little window in Crowley Hall's right tower.

The Order of the Owls was about to spring into action.

A small figure went down the stairs in Lizard Manor. Light steps echoed in the entrance hall, and the heavy door came open with a muffled creaking sound. A shadow sneaked outside, and a second later, a bicycle light pierced the darkness along the path that snaked down the cliff.

Silent as a shadow, the black bird followed Minerva to the village.

The bicycle suddenly braked to a halt in front of the post office, and the girl rolled on the ground.

"Ow!" a voice moaned. "You ran me over!"

Minerva realized that she had landed on Ravi. "I'm sorry," she whispered. "Why are you standing in the dark?"

"What kind of question is that?" He was quite annoyed. "To stay out of sight! Why do you think?"

Just then, another bike light popped up along Plum Avenue, and before Ravi and Minerva could make their presence known, Thomasina hit them squarely. "I didn't see you," the girl quickly apologized, straightening her bike.

"TCHEE-OOO!" came a call from the dark.

Ravi pricked up his ears. "Did you hear that?" he asked with worry.

But Minerva was simply too excited by the new adventure to listen to him. "Come on!" she urged. "We must leave before the sun comes up."

Ravi got on his old bike and started pedaling, but he kept listening carefully. His efforts were in vain, though, because the little black bird followed them through the village alleys in total silence.

They passed the school and the last houses, which were still shrouded in darkness. In a few minutes, they reached the spot where the river became deeper and the bike lights revealed old Jim's raft.

The kids hid their bikes behind a hedge and lit up a lantern Thomasina had brought from home. Then they threw their backpacks full of supplies, the camping gear, and the sleeping bags onto the raft.

Minerva was the first one to hop on the raft, which rocked a little under her weight. Old Jim had given her permission to use it, provided that she wouldn't go any farther than the point where the river entered the forest, because the currents grew very strong from there on.

"We'll be careful," Minerva had told him, which was not exactly a lie.

"All aboard!" the girl ordered once she had fixed the lantern to the main mast.

When they untied the raft and got away from the riverbank, the sun had not yet risen, but a thin strip of light started to appear on the horizon toward the ocean. Across the river, on the other hand, a light mist was rising from the ground, making it rather foggy.

The three friends set their gear at the center of the raft and tied it up with a piece of rope. Finally, they hoisted the sail.

Minerva pointed at the long push pole lodged in an oarlock on the bow. "We'll take turns operating the pole," she said. "Remember that Jim told us to always stay at an equal distance from both banks and look out for the rocks that surface from the bottom of the river."

For a while, they went along without any problems, sailing lightly on water that was as smooth as a mirror.

When Ravi's turn came, however, the wind roughed it up a little, raising tufts of mist. The boy looked at the surroundings with a bit of uneasiness. As they went on, the vegetation grew thicker and so did the silence. It was broken only by the gentle lapping of the water.

"We've never journeyed this far away from

Pembrose . . ." he muttered with a shaky voice. He cast other nervous looks at the riverbanks, and when he thought he had seen a bush move, he added, "Do you think there are boars in the forest?" He had heard someone say that there were such animals in the English woods.

Minerva and Thomasina were sitting at the bottom of the main mast, glancing around and staying close.

"If something happens, we can call the owls for help," Minerva said, looking at the small flute that she always carried around her neck. The flute was the amulet that Althea had left to her newborn baby girl. Minerva squeezed it, instantly feeling closer to her ancestor who had outsmarted her enemies and managed to put her hands on a magnificent treasure. She was suddenly flooded with courage. "We'll be all right," she said confidently.

Thomasina straightened the charming dress she was wearing, adjusted the elegant ribbon she had tied in her hair, and livened up. "And we'll find

Morgana —" she began. However, her voice died in her throat when the raft hit a rock. The blow shook the raft like a rag doll. "Ravi, you're worse than a freshwater sailor!" she grunted.

Hurt by that comment, the boy regained control of the raft and muttered, "I've got some experience now you know."

He had just spoken those words when disaster struck! The black bird with the red beak came out of nowhere, and Ravi panicked, dropping the pole. The strong currents sent the raft into a swirl.

"Let's row with our hands!" Minerva cried.

The friends put their arms into the water and tried to steady the raft and push it toward the riverbank, but they nearly fell every time the raft rocked.

"Hold on!" Minerva screamed.

It was pointless: the raft struck another rock with such violence that the three of them were hurled onto the shore, while the raft continued its crazy race down the river. Fortunately they broke their fall on a patch of fern.

Minerva was the first to get up. "Is everyone all right?" she asked her friends.

It seemed the scare had been greater than the damage, and the other two got on their feet.

"Gosh, what a blow!" Ravi mumbled, rubbing his bottom.

Minerva looked at the river. "We have to get the raft back," she said. "Maybe it'll run aground in a while." She took off running along the shore.

Ravi and Thomasina joined her in a desperate run, but the trees and plants were so thick that they were forced to slow down almost immediately. The raft soon disappeared from their sight, headed for who knows where.

"Oh, no," Ravi moaned. "Our supplies are gone!"

"And so are our sleeping bags . . . and our compass," said Thomasina, who had also lost her purse.

The three friends stopped and fell to their knees, panting and worried.

"What are we going to do now?" Ravi asked.

They were soaked to their bones, in the thick of

an unknown forest full of dangers. They had completely failed: their new adventure was over before it had even had the time to begin . . . with a shipwreck!

Minerva whipped the wet curls off her face so she could see clearly. "Well, we made it to the forest," she said, determined to find a bright side to the whole story. "That was our goal, wasn't it?"

"That's right," Thomasina agreed. She wrung out a heavy, soaked piece of skirt and added, "Even though I would have preferred to get here in a more elegant way." She sighed, scowling at Ravi. She had lost her pretty ribbon, and her wet hair now cascaded down her shoulders.

In the meantime, the sun had come up. It felt like it would be a hot day, which would take care of the wet clothes at least.

Minerva made a decision. "I think we should follow the path of the river to make sure that we don't get lost."

"You mean follow it toward home, don't you?" Ravi tried.

"Oh, no. I mean onward into the forest," Minerva said. "Don't tell me you want to give up now that we've come this far! We must find Morgana."

Something creaked somewhere, and Ravi jumped. "A boar!" he yelped, terrified.

But it was just a squirrel trying to pick up an acorn that was stuck between some dry leaves. Its whiskers whirring, it grabbed its loot and scurried off up a tree.

Thomasina laughed. "Wow, that was scary! Boy! Boars sure are frightening animals . . ."

Minerva raised her arm like a tour guide would do. "This way, please," she said, starting to walk along the edge of the river.

Sighing, Ravi followed her. He couldn't find the courage to remind her that they wouldn't last long without their supplies. After all, they weren't squirrels that could feed on acorns!

Following the river had seemed like a sensible idea, but putting it into practice wasn't possible. As if trying to keep people from doing that very thing, the trees kept growing thicker and thicker along the riverbank, and the kids were forced to take constant detours into the forest.

They soon lost sight of the river and couldn't reach it anymore.

"I knew it. We're lost." Ravi sighed, glancing

around. "Agatha warned us that the forest doesn't like intruders," he reminded them. "I wonder where it's leading us now."

Minerva was determined to find a way out of the situation, but she was starting to lose heart herself.

"Maybe the legend that Agatha told us about is

really true," Ravi insisted. "It feels like someone is watching me, like the trees are alive!"

"Same here . . ." Thomasina had to admit.

Even Minerva had felt it. All they could hear around them was the wind blowing between the branches, dry leaves rustling, and twigs snapping. Every now and then, however, she thought she had heard something else. But she didn't want to scare her friends. "I suggest going . . . that way!" she decided, pointing in a random direction, but saying it with so much confidence that she herself believed it was actually the right way.

So they went deeper and deeper in Rowan Forest. The landscape was quite different from the heath moor and the windswept coast they were used to. Here, the blinding light of the ocean was replaced by an endless dark green, interrupted here and there by rare puddles of light. The thick undergrowth made it hard to walk, and the three friends were constantly forced to climb over large fallen branches and rocks. It looked almost like no other human being had been there before them. Whenever they looked up, they felt tiny compared to the incredibly tall trees with their red bark, sticky with resin that filled the air with an unpleasantly sweet smell.

At a certain point, the trees closed in around them, as if trying to choke them.

Ravi froze in his steps. He had a lump in his throat. "I have that feeling again," he said nervously. "There's something here, I'm sure. Or maybe —" and the second option was even more frightening "— the trees are watching us!"

Thomasina had lost some of her boldness, but she didn't want to give up her adventure. "Come on! I'm sure there's no one here," she reassured him.

To prove her wrong, the heads of a wolf, a fox, and a bear suddenly popped up out of the thick of the woods.

That's who was keeping an eye on them; it wasn't the trees after all.

CHAPTER 5

THE SECRET OF
THE FOREST

The wolf, the fox, and the bear looked ready to fight, yet Ravi was quite relieved; he realized that they were nothing more than kids just like them, dressed up as animals.

The masks were very impressive. They were made of bits of bark, painted leaves, and cotton wads. Their fur was made with pieces of cloth. For the noses, they had used acorns and nuts and walnut shells, while their whiskers were made with bristles. The parts of the face and neck that were not covered by the

masks were painted in colored stripes, like some sort of warrior.

The six children stood face-to-face, looking at each other with a mixture of surprise and defiance. But the tension was soon broken by a little dormouse and a squirrel with blond pigtails.

"You got 'em!" the dormouse cried triumphantly.

"I knew they couldn't get away from us!" the squirrel echoed him in a shrill voice.

Puzzled, Minerva first looked at one and then shifted her eyes to the other. "Who are *you*?"

The wolf took a step forward. He was the tallest and seemed to be the leader of the odd gang. "Who are you?" he asked suspiciously.

"I think they're spies," said the fox in an obnoxious voice.

"We most definitely are not!" replied Minerva, offended.

"We are here to answer a request for help," Thomasina added, challenging the fox with the raise of her chin.

"Are you now?" the fox snapped snapped back, looking down on her. She had a mane of red hair, just like the coat of a real fox. "It seems to me like you are the ones who need help," she said.

"They're just a bunch of amateurs who got lost in the forest," said the bear.

"That's right! Take a look at their clothes," the fox said with a giggle. Thomasina turned red in the face and almost threw herself at the haughty fox.

Ravi held her back. "You're right. We did get lost, but we're not amateurs! We're the Order of the Owls." He'd let it slip then immediately fell silent, remembering that it was a secret.

"Never heard of that," said the fox curtly.

Minerva had had enough. She took the message she had found in the bottle out of the inside pocket of her jacket. Fortunately, it was dry. "We've come all the way from Pembrose because of this," she said, handing the scroll to the wolf, who was still sizing them up. "We found it in a bottle stuck in the sand on the edge of the river," she explained.

The five masked children studied the message with curious eyes and had a short discussion.

"I'm sorry. There is no Morgana in the forest," said the wolf at last, giving the message back to Minerva. He looked a tad less suspicious now.

"And we know this forest quite well!" the little dormouse said with an air of self-importance.

"It's too bad you've come all this way for nothing," the fox concluded with fake regret.

Thomasina flared up with anger. Never in her whole life had she met such a smug person!

"Why are you all so wet?" asked the squirrel, pointing at their clothes.

"We were sailing up the river on a raft," Minerva answered. "And . . . we shipwrecked."

"It was an accident," Ravi mumbled.

"What are you doing here?" Thomasina asked, looking daggers at the fox.

"We protect the forest!" the dormouse answered.

"Hush!" said the fox, giving him a nudge.

Minerva's curiosity, however, had taken off.

"Really?" she asked. "Is that the reason why you are masked?"

The wolf paused for a long while. Behind the mask, two dark and sharp eyes studied Minerva with uncertainty. The red-curled girl held his gaze with firmness.

"We come from Honey Combe," said the wolf at last. "A village on the opposite side of the forest from Pembrose." Minerva gave a sideways look at her friends, who answered back with a look of understanding. Honey Combe . . . the very same village that had received Merlin's punishment!

"Some of us live there," the wolf went on. "Others are just visiting on vacation."

The fox drew closer. "Don't tell them too much," she warned him.

He shook his head. "It's no secret anyway. Our mayor is very sick, and during his leave, his deputy, Mr. Turner, has taken advantage of a new law that allows the sale of state forests to private owners. To solve the town's financial problems, he decided to sell Rowan Forest to a crook from London. The guy's going to turn it into a luxury golf course. They're about to close the deal," he explained glumly.

"That's what *they* think!" the bear butted in.

The wolf sneered like a real one would. "Right, because we're going to stop him and save the forest!"

Minerva brightened up: maybe their adventure had begun badly, but it could be straightened out And who knows? Maybe if they remained in the forest in the company of experienced guides, eventually they could find out something more about Morgana. "Can we help you?" she asked impulsively. Only a moment later did she look at her friends to see if they agreed.

"Yes, as a matter of fact . . . we are rather experienced in these kind of missions," Thomasina said, looking defiantly at the fox.

Ravi felt yet another cramp in his stomach, which, on second thought, could have also been caused by the fact that they hadn't had breakfast yet. "Since we're here . . ." he muttered, somewhat reluctantly.

It seemed the wolf had made up his mind.

He finally lowered his mask and said, "My name's Conrad."

It wasn't easy to tell if Conrad was handsome, because his face was covered by two brown stripes. When he smiled, though, dimples formed in his cheeks. He had honest eyes and funny ears that stuck out of a thick mop of chestnut hair. "This is my gang," he said, pointing at the skeptical-looking group.

The dormouse was the first to come forward. "My name's Alex." He lowered his mask to reveal a little round face, sprinkled with freckles.

The pig-tailed squirrel was named Kitty, the bear was Jacob, and the fox was Anastasia. When Anastasia lowered her mask, Thomasina discovered that the girl was even more unbearable than she first thought; she had the kind of snub nose Thomasina had always dreamed of having herself.

The members of the Order of the Owls introduced themselves, and since Ravi had already mentioned it, they shared a few stories about their past adventures.

Conrad looked impressed and looked at them

with renewed interest. "If you promise that you'll keep it secret," he said at last, "we'll take you to a place that only we know about."

"We promise!" exclaimed Minerva.

Anastasia was quick to butt in. "I don't trust them," she hissed.

Thomasina burned with anger. "If you put it that way, I don't trust you either!" she cried, glaring at her.

Conrad put himself between the two. "We'll see who's right," he concluded in a soothing tone. "For the time being, follow us."

They walked on in single file. Anastasia and Jacob kept to themselves at the end of the line, as if to silently voice their protest. Conrad, on the other hand, was at the head of the line. He looked certain, like a real leader, and knew exactly where to go.

"How can you find your way without a compass?" Thomasina asked him.

"There are other ways," he said. "Like looking at the moss that grows on trees, for instance. Did you know that it points north? Or you can follow the dried up trail of streams."

Every now and then you could hear something calling: whistles and noises that made Ravi nervous. When a roar echoed in the air, he literally jumped. "Are there any dangerous animals here?" he asked Kitty, the squirrel, who was walking next to him.

She laughed. "Don't worry, that was Colin, one of our lookouts hidden in the treetops. He was just signaling that the coast is clear."

Indeed, the snout of a whiskered weasel poked out from the trees. "Hi!" he said.

Conrad made a gesture with his hand saying that everything was okay, and the weasel's face vanished back into the leaves.

"So it's not just the five of you?" Ravi asked Kitty.

"No, there are lots of kids from the village who have been helping us out," she replied.

"Nobody can stand Deputy Mayor Turner! That slimy maggot," Alex the dormouse grunted.

"How are you going to save the forest?" Minerva asked.

Conrad grew serious. "It's no easy feat, I'm warning you."

The girl smiled. "Oh, we like a challenge!"

"Sure we do . . ." Ravi mumbled, barely managing not to trip on a big root.

"This is one of Great Britain's oldest forests," Conrad explained. "Its trees came from oaks, beeches, and walnuts that grew here hundreds of years ago. They feed the undergrowth and animals. They make it possible for us to breathe and live. They are kind to humans, and those men want to destroy them!"

There was so much passion in the words of the gang's leader, that Minerva was won over. More and more curious about him, she tried to figure out how old he was. At least thirteen, she decided.

"That's a beech tree," said Conrad, pointing at a tall tree in front of them. Then he picked something up from the ground. It looked like a small triangular nut, wrapped up in what looked like a burr. "And this is its fruit, a beechnut." He put it in Minerva's hand.

She removed the shell and took a bite. "It's good!" she said, surprised. "It tastes a bit like a chestnut."

Ravi immediately went over to her. "What tastes like a chestnut?" he asked. It must have been the middle of the morning, and he still hadn't eaten breakfast.

Conrad scooped up a handful of beechnuts and gave them to Ravi. "Here you go. Enjoy!"

Ravi looked somewhat disappointed, but it was still better than nothing. He politely offered one to Thomasina and then scarfed down the rest.

They went on deeper into the forest, which took

on a totally different look now that they were with Conrad. Minerva was able to pick up details that she had missed before. The undergrowth, for example, was a sea of colored flowers: bellflowers, windflowers, daffodils. The air teemed with life: beetles, fireflies, ladybugs, and butterflies that shone whenever a ray of light touched them. They bumped into a wild hare that shot off like a rocket the moment it saw them, and they met a family of curious dormice.

Little by little, Ravi's mood improved as well, and he started to think that Rowan Forest had become their friend and didn't want to scare them off any more. However, a little sneeze was enough to drive him crazy with fear.

"TCHEE-OOO!"

"Oh no! It's him again!" the boy cried, looking up.

The small, red-billed bird fluttered in the middle of the group of kids, who stared at it in awe.

"What's he doing here?" asked Conrad.

"He's been following us since yesterday," Ravi complained, waving his arms to shoo him off.

He hadn't forgotten that it was the bird's fault he had lost control of the raft.

The kids of Rowan's gang looked at the little black bird with wonder.

"He's a Cornish chough," Conrad said. "A very rare bird. It usually never flies too far away from the coast, because it builds its nest on the cliffs. The locals consider it the region's symbol. It represents our proud and independent spirit."

In the meantime, the little bird seemed to be in the middle of a real dare with Ravi. The more the boy tried to wave it off, the closer the chough came to him, grazing him with its black wings, until it managed to land on the boy's shoulder, squeezing it with its little red feet.

Ravi turned to look at the bird and was met by two little lively black eyes. "Why do you keep bothering me?" he whispered.

Then he realized that Conrad and his friends were now looking at him with a new kind of respect. "Well? What is it?" he asked, puzzled.

"I've never seen anything like it!" Conrad exclaimed.

Jacob was amazed too. "Choughs never come close to anyone," he explained. "Only to the people they trust . . . *special* people." Ravi blushed. Everybody was looking at him as if he were some kind of hero — something he wasn't used to at all.

"I'd say this takes care of your doubts." Thomasina stepped in, making a face at Anastasia. "If the Cornish chough trusts us, you can too." She was so happy to have had the best of that mangy fox that she looked at Ravi with her eyes full of pride, melting him there on the spot.

"That's right," Conrad agreed. "I think it's convincing proof." He began to walk again, but he looked worried.

"What's wrong?" Minerva asked him.

"I don't know . . ." the gang leader replied, shaking his head. "The fact that the chough flew all the way over here is really strange. I'm wondering what might be the reason."

"As a matter of fact, it was him who led us to the bottle with Morgana's message," the girl said.

"Maybe he wants to help you find her," Conrad suggested. "Maybe you didn't come too late." He smiled at her. "In this place, anything is possible."

"*TCHEE-OOO!*" said the chough, and to Ravi's deep relief, it disappeared once again into the treetops.

Now he could enjoy Thomasina's smiles. He stood up straight and puffed out his chest. Could it be possible that his friend had finally understood what kind of person he was? Ravi was starting to think so.

It was a shame that he then tripped on a branch and ruined the magic.

CHAPTER 6

ROWAN'S OLD OAK

After walking for a good thirty minutes, the kids came to a clearing with a huge tree standing in the middle of it. "This is Rowan's millennial oak," said Conrad. "The oldest tree in the forest."

The three members of the Order of the Owls were amazed. The oak tree was huge and had a noble, grand look. The leaves were dark green, lush and shiny, and the branches were full of ripe acorns. The trunk was wrinkled and marked by time, covered with big spots of moss and little red mushrooms.

As Minerva walked closer to touch it with her hand, it occurred to her that if Agatha's legend was true, maybe, before being transformed by Merlin's spell, the tree had been a wise old man from the village of Honey Combe. Its presence gave one a sense of peace and courage.

"We are convinced that if someone cuts this oak tree down, the entire forest will die," explained Conrad, standing next to her. "The trees are connected through roots and branches, but there's also a secret stream that flows from tree to tree, keeping them all together."

"She's our guardian," said little Alex with a sigh, watching the oak tree with pride.

"It's hollow inside," Kitty's voice added. "She's also our house."

Minerva kneeled down and stuck her head into an opening that was just big enough for a child to squeeze through. She had expected the inside to be dark, but a beam of light seeped through from the other side of the trunk. She stepped in and immediately felt at home. The cavity was incredibly roomy and even furnished!

There were beds made of moss, a makeshift table built with pieces of bark and little chairs made out of tree stumps. The tree naturally formed shelves where supplies were laid out in orderly fashion. There were pans, plates, mugs, wooden cutlery, a copper cauldron, and baskets full of mushrooms, fruits, and berries. There were also tools, books, and even an accordion. The place was tied together by rust-colored rug made of leaves. A flight of natural steps went up the trunk, all the way to a landing that probably overlooked the entire forest.

Conrad went in after Minerva. "Do you like it?" he asked.

The girl took deep breaths to savor the pleasant smell of resin and moss. "Did you do this?" she asked, indicating the magical world that surrounded her.

"No, we found it all like this. Amazing, isn't it?"

Their voices boomed and echoed in the cavity as if they had been speaking through a funnel.

It feels safe here, Minerva thought. In that moment, something caught her attention — there was a small letter M carved into the wood above the small opening where they had entered. At least that was what it looked like to her. However, her investigation was interrupted by a series of whistles. "What's happening?" she asked Conrad.

The boy had an alarmed look on his face. "That's the curlew's bird call," he replied. "It's from Maya, the lookout posted up at the beginning of the clearing. It's the signal that someone's coming this way." He rushed out of the oak tree, followed by Minerva. "Let's go!" he yelled to his friends. Then he put on his animal mask, and the others did the same. "You can wait for us here," he said to Minerva.

"Not a chance!" the girl exclaimed. "We want to help you. What do we have to do?"

Conrad went back into the oak tree and came out with a bundle of thin bamboo straws. "Each of you take one and follow me."

The three members of the Order of the Owls had

no idea what the straws were for, but they did as the others and took one, asking no questions.

They walked out of the clearing, and Conrad and his friends made so much noise, stomping on branches and hitting the trees, that Minerva was not the least surprised when they found themselves face-to-face with two men.

"Oh, you have found us!" cried the boy with fake wonder. "You'll never get us, though!"

It occurred to Minerva that he was trying to keep them away from the big oak tree. Great idea, but how were they going to get away from those men? Running at breakneck speed, she followed him until they came to the riverbank.

"Oh no! We're trapped!" an alarmed Ravi said.

The men were still hot on their heels.

Just then, Minerva realized that there was a reed thicket in the river and Conrad's plan became clear to her. "Go in and stay underwater. Breathe through the straws," she whispered to Ravi and Thomasina.

They all dove into the river and hid among the

reeds. Minerva and Ravi found themselves facing each other, crouched at the bottom of the river. The girl saw her friend's face relax the moment he realized that he could breathe through the straw, and she smiled to encourage him.

After what felt like an eternity, Conrad peeked out of the water and signaled that the coast was clear. They reemerged, soaked to the bones, and took off their masks.

"You did a good job!" Conrad told them.

Thomasina wrung out her dripping dress and was disappointed to realize that there wasn't even one single wrinkle on Anastasia's.

"The lookouts give the alarm every time that someone gets too close to the big oak tree," Conrad told them. "So we find a distraction to drive away the intruders. Usually, the best solution is to lead them to the river."

"They haven't figured out the straw trick yet." Kitty laughed.

Conrad looked at his new friends with respect.

"You know what? You earned the right to become honorary members of Rowan's gang. Are you in?"

"Of course we are!" Minerva cheered proudly.

Ravi wondered if being part of two secret gangs would mean a few too many adventures and the dangers that came with them. But he didn't have time to ponder that for too long because, to his great delight, Thomasina took his arm and passed Anastasia, raising her chin and splashing her with water.

Once they were back in the clearing, Ravi, Minerva, and Thomasina were sworn in as honorary members of Rowan's gang through a very serious initiation ceremony. All three took the oath in unison: *I say and promise hereby / respect to trees I shall not deny. / Oak, ash, and buckthorn / shall fill with courage every newborn!*

"Now you have to choose the name of a forest animal," Alex said.

"Oh, I already know!" Minerva smiled. "I'll be the owl."

Thomasina looked at Anastasia, thinking hard to

find an animal that would be prettier and smarter than the one she had chosen. "I'll be the lynx!" she decided. And she almost added, *Which could eat a fox in one single mouthful.*

"There are no lynxes in Cornwall," Anastasia complained.

Thomasina shrugged. "So what? They still live in forests."

Ravi couldn't make up his mind: hunger cramps made it impossible for him to think.

"What about the hare?" Minerva suggested, winking at him. "It runs fast when it smells danger."

"Oh, well . . . all right," Ravi mumbled. "How about a snack now?"

* * *

The moment he realized that all they would be eating were things found in the forest, Ravi plunged into deep despair: wild fruits, berries, nuts, mushrooms, acorn flour, and beechnuts hadn't sounded particularly inviting to him.

Kitty the squirrel was the gang's cook. "I bet you're gonna ask for seconds," she said, handing him a bowl of gross-colored slop dotted with purple berries that looked like lumps.

I doubt it, Ravi thought with a sigh. However, not only did he have two helpings of that dish, he also ate three pieces of walnut cake and gulped down at least half a gallon of wild blueberry juice.

"You're making us look bad," Thomasina whispered to him when he used his hand to wipe his mouth. Good manners were of the utmost importance for her, even in the forest.

"Oh, leave me alone, will you? I haven't even had lunch today!" he replied, rubbing his stomach.

When their feast was over, guarded by the presence of the great oak tree, Conrad told them about their struggle with Deputy Mayor Turner. "So far, we have just been hassling the officials that come here to survey the land and take measurements for the golf course," he admitted. "But we need a solid plan to save the forest."

Minerva scratched her nose. "What does the mayor say about this? He's got more power than Turner, doesn't he? Did you try asking him for help?"

A shadow passed across Conrad's face. "Mayor Briar has never agreed to sell the forest," he replied. "But he's very sick, and he's staying at a hospital that's out of town. He has such a high fever that he's rarely conscious. That's how Turner took over."

"What about your parents?" Ravi interjected. "Why aren't they helping you?"

"They don't like the idea of the golf course," Jacob answered. "But they can't protest because the law is on the deputy mayor's side."

"Besides, some people are already dreaming of making a fortune off of it," Anastasia continued. "A golf course will bring in people who will need accommodations and food and who will spend money in the town stores.

"So even our parents are ready to sacrifice the forest," Conrad sighed. "However, since they feel guilty, they have been turning a blind eye to our activities.

All in all, they think it's only a game that will soon have to stop."

Minerva thought that the kids had far more guts than the grown-ups. She felt a great admiration for Conrad and his friends who, against the odds, were fighting to keep their hopeless case alive.

"We go home in the evening, and we come back here in the day," Conrad resumed. "But someone's always here watching the great oak tree. We don't want anybody to find it."

"How are you planning to stop Turner?" Minerva asked.

"We don't know yet," Conrad admitted. "For the moment, we're trying to buy some time until the mayor gets better. He's a good man. He taught me all I know about the trees and nature. However, he's lost his courage as he's gotten older," he added. "I'd like to tell him that if the village needs money, there are other ways. We could try environment-friendly tourism. We should be planting new trees to make our forest more beautiful, not destroying it!"

They all stood in silence, brooding over the problem.

"There's also a mystery here, you know," said Kitty, giving Ravi the last slice of walnut cake.

Minerva pricked up her ears. "A mystery?"

"We found some strange objects hidden in the hollows of the tree trunks," an excited Alex said. "And a map too!"

Minerva exchanged a look with her friends. "Can I see it?" she asked.

The little boy went into the oak tree and came back holding a scroll, which he unrolled in front of the girl. It was a map of the forest, drawn on a couple of dozen leaves sewn together.

"It was drawn using the juice of a red berry that grows only in Rowan," Conrad said.

Minerva took out the message that she had found in the bottle and held it next to the map.

"Wow! They're the same leaves!" her new friend exclaimed. "I didn't notice when you showed the message to me earlier."

"Even the ink is exactly the same," Ravi observed.

Minerva studied the map closely: the river, the trees, the flowers, and the little plants in the undergrowth were drawn down to every detail, as if an artist had done it, and some of them were marked with colored dots. There were no words written on it, not even the name of the author.

"Do you think Morgana did this?" Thomasina asked her friend.

"I don't know." Minerva shook her head, doubtful. "Maybe. Are you sure you've never heard of her? Not even in your village?" she asked the children from Honey Combe. "We think she's a girl who lost her parents . . ." she went on explaining. Then she seemed to have suddenly remembered something and darted into the oak tree yelling, "Follow me!" When they were all inside the tree, Minerva pointed at the *M* cut into the wood above the opening. "I saw it earlier. Did one of you carve it?" she asked.

Conrad shook his head. "No. Everything is just the way we found it."

"Then that could stand for Morgana!" Minerva guessed. She looked around and added, "What if she built this hideout?"

"You're right," Thomasina said. "Maybe she came to live in the forest when her parents died. Perhaps she used to live in one of the villages around here."

Minerva ran a hand through her curly hair and considered the idea. "What does the map show?" she finally asked the leader of Rowan's gang.

"It's a survival map," Conrad replied. "The dots show fruits, berries, leaves, and edible mushrooms."

"And that's not all," Alex whispered. He stood on his toes to take a basket that was on a high shelf and put it on the table. First, he took out a lock of black hair tied with a ribbon. Minerva took it and turned it over in her hand. Where had she seen that kind of hair before . . . black with purple highlights, just like heather in the night?

Alex fished out more troves: a white cotton baby dress with flowers embroidered on the hem. A bonnet as green as spring grass. Crocheted wool shoes.

"And here it says what kind of leaves shine at night, the ones you can use to find your way," Jacob said, handing Minerva a small book.

The girl studied it. Its cover was made of bark, while the pages were leaves sewn together. Tiny writing in red ink filled every space available.

"It also contains the recipes for my dishes," Kitty chimed in.

"And it explains how to make an ointment for insect bites," Alex butted in. "That came in pretty handy when I stepped into a wasp nest."

Minerva studied every item, her eyes filled with

amazement. Did Morgana leave these things in the forest? And why had she hidden them in the tree?

When the children were getting ready for the night, the red-curled girl was still mulling over the mystery. Conrad built a small bonfire by the great oak tree and roasted beechnuts and chestnuts. The air was soon filled with the crackling sound of burning wood and an inviting smell.

Thomasina and Ravi were helping Conrad, putting the roasted fruits in the plates. The other members of Rowan's gang had already gone back home, leaving a feeling of lonesomeness behind.

Minerva looked intently at the flame, lost in her own thoughts. "We must find out what happened to Morgana," she said at last, holding the small bark and leaves book that she had read from cover to cover. "Maybe we can still help her." Even though Agatha thought otherwise, she hadn't given up hope yet.

"That's right!" Thomasina agreed, relishing the thought of showing Anastasia that they hadn't come too late.

Ravi, on the other hand, was worried. He really wished he had a lair to hide out in, just like the hare he had taken his name and mask from. The forest scared him now that the night had fallen: the branches were withered arms, talons reaching out for him. He hadn't forgotten Agatha's words about the trees starting to walk one day — and they seemed to be getting closer whenever he had the courage to look at them. Actually, one was closing in that very moment. Then he heard a kind of sneezing sound and realized that his winged friend had returned.

The chough popped out of the foliage, and to Ravi's great disappointment, landed right on his shoulder.

"Do you think I'm your perch?" the boy grunted.

Conrad smiled. "You know, some people think King Arthur keeps on living in the body of a chough."

"What?" said a surprised Ravi, turning to face the bird's small glittering eyes.

"The old mayor told me," Conrad explained. "When Arthur was fatally wounded in the battle of Camlann, his spirit migrated into the body of a chough. The red legs and beak represent the wounds he sustained in battle. Since then, Arthur has been living in Cornwall, the land he loved more than anything else. As long as there are choughs in the world, there will always be hope that one day the mythical king will recover his human form."

Ravi studied the little leg that was squeezing his shoulder. "Arthur, is that you?" he asked softly, looking into the cunning eyes with renewed interest.

"TCHEE-OOO!" cried the chough. Then it opened its black wings and took off, once again vanishing among the trees.

"He seems to be partial to you," said Conrad.

"That's right. I'm sure he'll soon make you a Knight of the Round Table!" Minerva chimed in.

Ravi straightened his back and puffed out his chest. "Knight, no less," he said in a solemn tone.

"Sir Ravi, Knight of the Hare!" Thomasina shouted, laughing.

CHAPTER 7

SLEEPING BEAUTIES IN THE WOODS

The four kids slept like logs inside the belly of the great oak tree, and the following morning they were awakened by the sweet smell of chestnut fritters.

Kitty and Alex had arrived early from the village and had set to work, preparing everything they needed for breakfast on a tablecloth they had laid out on the grass in the clearing.

Jacob was blowing on the fire, while Anastasia poured blueberry juice into the wooden cups.

"This is wonderful!" Ravi sighed, as he helped

himself to a huge stack of hot fritters. He drowned them in maple syrup and thought that life in the forest had begun to grow on him, especially when the sun was high in the sky.

Minerva's hair was as messy and tangled as a blackberry bush, and her face was sleepy: she hadn't stopped thinking about how to save the forest for one single moment, not even in her sleep.

"We have a surprise for you!" Jacob announced suddenly.

Alex fetched a bundle and unfolded it, unveiling three masks: an owl, a lynx and a hare. "We made them last night," he said, handing them to the new friends.

"Now you are really part of our team!" Kitty clapped her hands.

"Oh, thank you!" exclaimed a delighted Minerva.

"That is very kind of you," Thomasina said with her usual grace.

Conrad smiled. "We only wear them when intruders come into the forest," he explained. "But they are our trademark, so we thought you would each like to have one."

"We like them a lot!" Minerva exclaimed. She immediately put hers on, tying it up behind her head with a thin piece of thread. "How do I look?" asked a voice muffled by a yellow beak made out of peanut shells. Then she jerked her head left and right and imitated the cry of the owls that lived behind her house. *"Woot! Woot!"*

"And how do I look?" Thomasina asked. Her mask was made of cotton that was as soft as real fur, and she had small pointy ears and long black whiskers.

"You look like a mangy cat," Anastasia muttered under her breath. The girl from Rowan's gang looked quite lovely, and her hair was tied back with a green ribbon Thomasina was rather jealous of, especially since she had lost hers.

"Don't listen to her," Kitty whispered. "She actually spent half the night sewing." She pointed at her friend's fingers, which were covered in bandages. "And she's not that good at it."

Thomasina didn't have time to wonder why Anastasia had been so kind to her because she was distracted by Ravi. He had put on his hare mask, and the long ears, made out of the sleeves of an old sweater, flapped up and down at his every move, cracking everybody up.

"I've never seen a knight with ears that long!" Minerva giggled.

Once they had cleared the table, the children shared their morning tasks: Kitty and Alex would wash the dishes in the river, then pick up supplies for lunch. The rest of the gang would patrol the forest.

Minerva quickly adapted to life in the forest: she climbed trees like a monkey, she was able to catch every sound and every rustle, and she had a strong nose for danger. She won over the members of Rowan's gang by making them each a slingshot and teaching them how to use it.

Unfortunately, during all those activities, she couldn't think of one single way to snatch the forest from the deputy mayor's greedy hands. There was no time to waste, though; the Order of the Owls had to be back home by Monday.

In addition, there was also Morgana's mystery to solve. After lunch Minerva sat against the trunk of the great oak tree, in the cooling shade of its thick canopy, and began to study the small book with the bark cover, looking for some clues.

The peace that reigned in the clearing, however,

was soon shattered by a girl's desperate screams. She must have been running for a long while, because she was almost out of breath when she finally stopped in front of Minerva. "Where's Conrad?" she asked.

The boy, who was gathering wood for the fire, had heard her and came running. The two talked for a while, then she went back the same way she had come from.

"That was Hatty," Conrad said. "An informer from the village. A team of agronomists are on their way. They're coming to survey the forest, and they're headed right here."

"How many are there?" asked Jacob, who had rushed over with the rest of the gang.

"At least four, unfortunately," Conrad replied. "I don't think the river trick will work this time." He ran a hand through his dark hair. He seemed more nervous than usual.

"But what are we going to do then?" Ravi asked.

"Why don't you use your chough to call for help?" Anastasia suggested sarcastically.

Thomasina felt a renewed sense of dislike for the girl with the thick red hair. "Why don't you keep your mouth shut for once?" she snapped at her.

The children from the gang began to nervously discuss the situation.

"Do we have to get our things?" Kitty asked.

"Are they going to cut down our oak tree?" Alex asked on the verge of tears.

Minerva clenched her fists. There had to be something she could do. She lowered her eyes upon the little book that she still held in her hand. The pages were filled with remedies, and she had read them all. Her freckled face lit up. "I've got an idea!" she cried.

The rest of them suddenly fell silent.

"Alex, get eight bamboo straws," Minerva ordered. "Kitty, put a pot of water on the fire. We'll make a brew. Everyone else, help me find these leaves," she said, showing them a page in the book.

"What kind of leaves are those?" Anastasia asked, smiling. "Do you want to offer a cup of hot relaxing tea to the agronomists?"

"Not exactly," the red-curled girl said. "This is not the kind of brew you drink. It's the kind you rub on your eyes. Here it says that it makes you fall asleep in a matter of seconds. Come on! Let's get to work!"

They quickly picked up handfuls of leaves that Kitty boiled into a thick and greenish slop. Then they poured it into small flasks that the children hung around their necks.

"All you have to do is suck a little bit of liquid into the straws," Minerva explained. "Don't worry if you swallow some of it, it won't hurt you. You'll spray it into the intruder's eyes. Don't miss!"

Minerva wore her owl mask with great excitement. *Woot! Woot!* was her battle cry.

Ravi the hare looked rather embarrassed, while Thomasina the lynx looked ferocious with her great feline whiskers. The three friends were now real members of Rowan's gang.

The children set up post in the treetops along the edge of the clearing. They were positioned so that every single access point to the clearing could be

watched. They soon heard a whistle from far away: one of the lookouts had given the alarm.

"Get ready, they're coming!" Conrad said from the highest branch of a beech.

The moment the agronomists arrived, the air was filled with hissing sounds. Not all of the children hit the target at the first shot, but a couple of minutes later the four men fell to the ground fast asleep.

"Hooray!"

"It worked!"

"The effect will last a couple of hours at least," Minerva said, letting herself slide down the trunk of the pine tree up which she had climbed.

"All we have to do now is drag them as far as possible from here," Conrad decided.

They took them to a little valley on the eastern edge of the forest in a quiet, sheltered place.

"No one will upset their sleep," said the leader of the gang with a sly smirk.

* * *

Despite their success, the kids didn't feel happy at all that night. They knew that the deputy mayor's officials were going to show up more and more often and in greater and greater numbers. They also knew that they couldn't fend them off forever.

"We need a real plan," Minerva said. *"Now."* There were four of them left, like the previous night, and Conrad had just finished building the fire. "We'll have go back home on Monday," the girl added.

"Because my parents will be back from Scotland and Mrs. Flopps will be back from Truro," Thomasina explained. Since she didn't have a ribbon, she had put a pink flower in her hair and felt pleasantly tired. Ravi had never seen her so beautiful.

Conrad sat down and put his hands close to the

fire. "I'm sorry you have to leave so soon," he said with a sigh.

"We're sorry we couldn't be of any real help," Ravi said with sincere regret.

"And we didn't even help Morgana." Minerva moaned. It wasn't like her to feel that disheartened, but the idea of soon having to say goodbye to Rowan's gang and the friendly presence of the great oak tree was almost unbearable.

"I'd like to show old Mayor Briar that not all is lost," said Conrad as he rekindled the fire. "I don't have a dad, and my mom works the whole day, so the mayor used to spend a lot of time with me. He's the one who first took me on trips to the forest and taught me to respect the environment and the plants. They breathe and feed just like humans, you know? And they suffer if we hurt them. This forest is alive!"

"Just like Agatha says," Ravi commented, remembering the words of the witch from the heath moor.

Minerva realized that she hadn't told Conrad that story yet. So she told him the ancient legend of Arthur, Merlin, and the trees that would one day wake up.

"It's rather curious that the story is about Honey Combe of all places," Thomasina said. "Conrad, did you know about the legend?"

"There are many rumors about Rowan and the neighboring villages," the boy replied. "And as a matter of fact, the mayor told me this story a long time ago," he recalled. He stared at the fire, and the flame illuminated his dark eyes. "It's nice to think that at one time, the people from my village had the courage to fight for what they believed in."

"Yes, but they were punished in a terrible way for their fight," Ravi chimed in.

"But they didn't stand and stare," Conrad insisted. "They didn't bow before injustice."

They kept talking, and as Minerva's eyelids grew heavier and heavier, an idea started to take shape inside her curly head. After sleep became too strong for her to resist and her eyes closed, she wished she would still remember it the following day.

CHAPTER 8

THE FINAL CHALLENGE

"Wake up lazybones!" Alex yelled.

The four children opened their eyes wide and realized they had fallen asleep by the great oak tree. They had been so tired the night before that they hadn't had the energy to go lay on the cozy moss beds inside the tree.

"We've been up since dawn, you know!" said Kitty. Under her arm she was holding a bundle that gave off the irresistible smell of freshly baked bread.

Anastasia and Jacob were scooping the ashes out of the fire pit. Minerva sat up all of a sudden and ran a hand through her unkempt hair. She had the feeling she should be remembering something important. Kitty, however, didn't give her time to think and dragged her away to help with breakfast. Then one chore quickly followed the next, and so the feeling dissolved just like the light, early morning mist that rises up from the undergrowth.

In the afternoon, the kids decided to go down to Honey Combe to spy on the enemy.

"The best defense is a good offense," Conrad had said, leading the gang.

The moment they emerged from the woods, Minerva was surprised to set her eyes on delightful round hills. The scene was very different from the jagged cliffs she was used to back home. Honey Combe was a charming village, nestled in a valley dotted with meadows and little thatched houses.

Before entering the village, they passed the small hospital where Mayor Briar was staying. Conrad pointed at a muscular man who was guarding the entrance. "Turner hired him," he whispered.

"Yeah. When the mayor wakes up, he'll immediately go tell Turner," Anastasia said.

"And he would immediately spill the beans if we tried to go see the mayor ourselves," added Jacob.

A window was open on the second floor, and soft winds ruffled white curtains. Other than this pleasant breeze, it was a sweltering day.

"That's his room," Jacob said. "He's so close . . . but we can't reach him."

The man at the entrance noticed them and gave them a threatening look.

"Come on, let's go," Conrad whispered. "Before he decides to tell Turner that we're here."

Sheltered by the hedges that surrounded lovely flowered lawns, the kids reached the deputy mayor's home. It was the most luxurious house in town, with a large, well-kept rose garden and wide windows that stood open to let in the fresh air.

Led by Conrad, the children crawled through the roses and waited quietly under the living-room windowsill.

"I'm sick and tired of those pests!" thundered a voice inside the house, making them all jump.

"That's him — Turner," Conrad whispered.

"I won't let a bunch of brats put a spoke in my wheel!" the deputy mayor continued.

"But there's nothing we can do," an edgy voice replied. "They're just kids . . ."

"Psh! Kids, my foot!" Turner growled. "They're smart, I tell you! I'm running out of patience, though. I've decided to act, Mr. Potting."

"Potting is the guy who wants to build the golf course," Alex whispered.

Conrad made a sign to hush and listened.

"Our mayor has woken up, unfortunately . . . I mean . . . well, you know what I mean," Turner corrected himself, clearing his throat. "And he's feeling rather well too. He'll be out of the hospital soon, so there's no time to waste."

"I already told you that I'll sign the contract only when I see the dozers in action and the first tree cut down," Potting said in an annoyed tone. "You have already made too many promises you didn't keep, my dear deputy mayor! I want to see the trees cut down with my own eyes. Only then will I shell out the money we agreed on. And a little something extra under the table for your help in the matter."

"What a slimy worm!" Kitty hissed. Conrad covered her mouth with his hand, but he too had a disgusted look on his face. Minerva felt her curls boil:

Turner was really as greedy and despicable as they had described him!

"I know, my dear Potting. Don't get worked up," the deputy mayor said. His tone was mellow now. "Listen to what I have in mind. I'll start the dozers tomorrow at dawn, while everybody is still sleeping. You'll see the first tree cut down, just like you asked."

"Are you serious, Turner?" There was a tinge of greedy hope in the Londoner's voice.

"Dead serious." The deputy mayor cackled evilly. "At that point, with the work already started, even the naysayers will have to give up. And I will hound out those pestering kids that hide in the forest!"

"You haven't been able to do that so far," the other man pointed out.

"This time they won't be able to ruin my plans!" the deputy mayor thundered. "I'll show those brats!"

The eight children exchanged looks, and Alex almost climbed up the windowsill to go tell that slimeball Turner what he thought of him. Jacob had to hold him back by the legs.

"Meet me tomorrow at four by Karnach stone, where the forest begins." They heard the creaking sound of armchair springs relaxing.

"All right, Turner, I want to trust you. I'll be there, and I'll have the money with me."

Steps echoed through the house, and Conrad made a gesture to his friends to go. The two men would show up at the main door any moment, and they couldn't risk being discovered.

Crawling on the grass and hidden by the hedges and bushes, they went back the same way they had come in and stopped only when they were once again in the safety of the forest clearing.

They were so nervous that for a while they spoke only about how evil Turner was, without so much as a single idea on how to stop him.

Inside Minerva's head, however, something had just started working itself out again. She was sitting at her favorite place, leaning against the trunk of the great oak tree. She gazed at the surrounding trees, feeling a burning desire to save them. In that moment, she saw a little sparrow, holding a bough in his beak, land on a beech tree branch in front of her, and the last piece of the puzzle finally found its place.

"You guys! I've got it!" she cried, springing to her feet.

The other children looked anxiously at her. Totally unflustered by the confusion that she had created, she started walking in circles with her hands behind her back. "Darn! I should've remembered earlier . . ."

"Minerva, are you okay?" Ravi asked.

She stopped and smiled that wily smile her friends knew so well. "Never been better, because . . ." Her smile grew wider. ". . . now I know that the trees can give us a hand!"

"Huh?" a surprised Conrad said. "But . . . how?"

"I'll explain everything in a while. Now there is very urgent business we have to take care of," Minerva replied excitedly. "First of all, we have to tell the mayor to be in front of Karnach stone tomorrow at four in the morning. According to Turner, he woke up, and he's feeling quite well."

"But how are we gonna tell him without the deputy mayor finding out?" Anastasia asked. "There's a man at the door."

"That's right . . ." Minerva thought about it. "Got it! We'll use a slingshot to send him a message through the open window. We'll just have to wrap it around a stone," she said. "We'll need a good shot for that. Alex can you do it?"

"Oh, yeah!" he answered full of enthusiasm and ran off to carry out the order.

"The second step is to get help from every kid in Honey Combe and the neighboring villages and ask them to meet us here in the clearing at three in the morning. Nobody must see them!" Minerva continued. "That should give us enough time to set everything up," she thought aloud.

Conrad looked at her, trying to figure out what she had in mind. Finally, he decided to trust her. "Kitty, Anastasia, Jacob, go and spread the word to all the kids. Tell them to come to the clearing, but tell them to follow only those who really know the way."

When the three children had gone, the leader of the gang turned to Minerva. "Will you tell us your plan now?"

Minerva realized that Ravi and Thomasina were also anxiously staring at her: they knew something big was brewing, but they still didn't know what she had in mind.

"Do you remember what Agatha told us?" she asked her friends. "One day, when confronted with another terrible injustice, Rowan's trees will awaken and start walking." A big grin shined on her freckled face. "The trees will defeat Turner. Then no one will ever be able to cut them down!"

Ravi shook his head. "How can you be so sure that the trees will walk for *real*?"

"That's right. Why now?" Thomasina added.

"Bringing an entire forest back to life is not an easy task," Conrad said.

"I know," replied Minerva. "But I'll try my best to do it!"

The other three didn't know what to think, but

the determined look on their friend's face had almost convinced them.

"Who's with me?" asked the girl as she put her hand forward.

"I'm in!" Thomasina said enthusiastically and put her hand on top of Minerva's.

Ravi and Conrad exchanged a look. "We are too," the older one said. And they both placed a hand on the girls'.

"I say and promise hereby / respect to trees I shall not deny. / Oak, ash, and buckthorn / shall fill with courage every newborn!" Minerva recited in a clear voice.

The other three repeated it after her, and they felt like Rowan's oath had given them an energy boost. "We're going to do it. You'll see!" said Minerva, full of conviction. "Before I give you the full story, however, there's still something missing."

She slipped through the narrow opening in the oak tree, and standing on her toes, she took the book with the bark cover out of the basket where it was stashed. She flipped through it until she found the page she was looking for. At that point, she smiled. "Thank you, Morgana!" she whispered with a wistful warmth in her eyes. "Without you, I would have never found the way . . ."

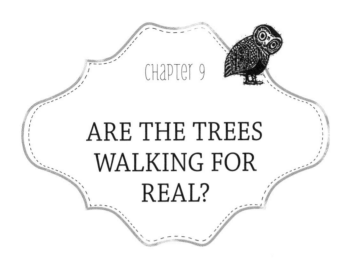

CHAPTER 9

ARE THE TREES WALKING FOR REAL?

Everything was set for Minerva's great plan. Jacob, Anastasia, and Kitty came back to the clearing shortly before six, saying that by sundown every kid in the neighboring villages would know about the meeting. A minute later, Alex arrived too, announcing that he had succeeded in throwing the message into the mayor's room.

"I ran before the thug at the door could see me," he reported to Minerva.

"Very good!" the girl said. She was wearing an apron that fell under her feet and was stirring something awfully stinky in the copper cauldron. Thomasina was keeping an eye on the flame. If they didn't keep the fire lit, the mush would turn completely solid.

Ravi and Conrad were picking up branches and leaves, which they then dropped on a pile in the middle of the clearing.

"Come help us!" the leader of the gang called to the others. "We must gather as much as we can."

When it was dark, they lit the lanterns they had made with hollowed out gourds and laid them around the oak tree. The tree had never looked as magical as it did that night.

Children started to arrive in small groups led by those who knew the way. Then the groups started to get bigger, until the whole clearing was fully packed.

When they were all there, Minerva told them about her plan to bring the ancient Rowan Forest back to life in order to defeat Deputy Mayor Turner.

At first, there were many bewildered whispers, but by the time Minerva had finished talking, the kids were won over and ready to help. They all took Rowan's oath aloud, in order to make the pact official. And so, under the loving gaze of the great oak tree, after more than one thousand years, Honey Combe's destiny was once again about to change.

* * *

It wasn't dawn yet, but a feeble light was beginning to make the lower part of sky lighter. The light was so tiny and quivering that it looked like someone had lit a candle. However, the sky was no longer black, but a marvelous blue, as soft as velvet.

In contrast, the forest looked like a black and indistinct mass to the deputy mayor, Mr. Potting, and the bulldozer operators. Even old Mayor Briar, who had accepted Minerva's invitation, saw it that way, and he felt a chill run down his spine.

"Hey, the trees are moving!" the man driving the bigger dozer suddenly cried.

"What?" Turner exclaimed. A stocky man, he was wearing a tie that squeezed his bull-like neck and seemed to be choking him. The moment he looked over at Rowan Forest, the deputy mayor felt like he was choking for real. "That's not possible!" he croaked.

But the trees were indeed moving toward Honey Combe, slowly but steadily, like an orderly and deadly army.

"I'll be darned!" cried Potting, scared out of his mind. Meanwhile the workers jumped off the bulldozers and ran for their lives.

Propped on a cane, the old mayor watched the spectacle with his mouth open wide. Getting there had been quite an effort for him, but it had definitely been worth it.

"Turner, what is this all about?" asked Mr. Potting with a shrill voice. "Is it part of your plan?"

The deputy mayor was desperately trying to loosen his tie, but all he managed was to make it even tighter. "Of course not!" he grunted. "I didn't authorize any of this!" He turned to the foreman, the only worker who hadn't left. "Did you do this?"

"I know nothing about this, sir," babbled the poor man, his hands clasped around his hard hat.

"This is outrageous!" barked a furious Potting. "I knew I shouldn't trust a simple villager like yourself. Back in London, we are serious about our business deals!"

As the people from Honey Combe came running, alarmed by the worker's screams, the forest trees kept marching on, waving their leafy branches. The shadows were still so thick, that you couldn't tell one from the other.

At that point, a deep, powerful voice thundered. "People of Honey Combe, we the trees of Rowan Forest have decided to awaken and rise against injustice! Know ye that we will not let you cut us down to build a golf course, hence forsake your plan now and forever!"

By then, Mr. Potting's eyes were popping out of his head. In an angry gesture, he took the contract he had kept ready in the inside pocket of his jacket and tore it up in front of Turner. "Here's what I can do with your promises, deputy mayor of bonehead land!" And he strode away, swearing that never again in his life would he set foot in the countryside. "Trees that walk!" he mumbled. "Ridiculous!"

"Potting, don't leave like this!" cried a desperate Turner as he ran after him. "We can still make a deal! Wait up . . ."

In the meantime, it looked like the forest didn't want to stop. It was still cloaked in darkness and kept moving at a steady pace. The branches and the leaves were shaking harder and harder.

Mayor Briar leaned firmly on his cane. He was an old man, and he had seen many things during his long life. But this spectacle beat it all. He remembered the legend about Rowan's trees well, and he knew that there is always a little bit of truth in every legend. In spite of his age, however, he had very good eyesight. He had seen something that had made him wonder. Besides, he knew of no tree that could throw messages through windows.

He smiled, imagining what had happened. This

time it had been just a warning, but who knows what would happen the next time. That spectacle had filled him with new energy. Selling the forest had seemed unavoidable to him, like progress, but now he was willing to fight again.

He raised his cane into the air and cried. "Rowan's trees, stop! I give you my word that no one will cut you down." He turned to his fellow citizens, who were watching from a distance. "Do you agree with me?"

Muttering rose among the people of Honey Combe, which then turned into distinguishable voices of consent. They all promised that the forest would never again be threatened.

"Did you hear that, Rowan's trees?" the mayor cried. "You can now go back to enjoying the peace of the forest. No one will ever dare hurt you again. Continue your slumber until another injustice wakes you." He lowered his cane and gave a bow.

Before everybody's astonished eyes, the trees began to retreat. Slowly, they moved back to where the forest had stood still for hundreds of years.

When the sun's round and dazzling sphere appeared above the leafy branches, Rowan's trees were slumbering once again.

* * *

Music, singing, and wild dancing! The old oak tree had never seen so much happiness and feverish activity in her entire life. The children of Honey Combe were celebrating the crushing victory over Deputy Mayor Turner. Alex was an accomplished accordion player, while Minerva and Conrad had turned out to be skilled dancers. Holding each other's arms, Anastasia and Thomasina twirled as if there had never been so much as a pinch of rivalry between them, while Ravi, also known as the Knight of the Hare, danced like a madman in the middle of the clearing, cracking everybody up as he shook his flapping ears.

All the kids had painted their faces green, and they had glued branches and leaves to their clothes, which made them look like young forest trees.

"Ah, I knew I would find you here!" a voice cried.

The music stopped all of a sudden, and the dancers froze in their steps. You could hear a pin drop.

The mayor of Honey Combe limped forward with a young woman of rare beauty at his side.

"Agatha!" yelled Minerva as she ran up to her. "What are you doing here?"

The witch from the heath moor hugged her tight, making her disappear under a waterfall of black hair. "Minerva Mint, I should be very mad at you!"

Ravi and Thomasina came forward with a sorry look on their faces. In contrast, Minerva didn't look sorry at all. "I *had* to answer Morgana's request for help," she justified, looking at Agatha from the bottom up.

The young woman sighed. "I know, my dear." To the girl's great surprise, she hugged her one more time. "When I didn't see you in Pembrose, I knew you had come here." She shook her head. "I should have known that my words wouldn't have been enough to stop you. You were gone for so long that I started to worry and came looking for you," she explained. "And when I arrived in Honey Combe, I witnessed an incredible thing."

"Did you see the trees walk?" Ravi and Thomasina asked in unison.

"You could say that!" the mayor said. Then he turned to Conrad.

The boy was wearing his wolf mask and had kept to himself since the mayor had arrived, as if he had been afraid that the man would be upset with him.

"And I also saw a mask I made with my own hands and gave to a dear friend," the mayor continued. "That's when I knew who had masterminded the whole thing." He smiled. "I know I have been an old fool, but I promise you from now on, we'll fight together for this forest. Deal?"

Conrad, the fearless wolf, seemed on the brink of tears, but he pulled himself together and shook the hand that the man had offered him. "Deal," he replied.

Briar was so happy that he felt like he didn't even need his cane anymore. He leaned on his young friend's shoulder. He looked at the painted faces of the children of his town and asked, "Who's going to tell me how you managed to wake up Rowan's trees?"

"Oh, that was easy," Minerva promptly replied. "As a matter of fact, Agatha gave me the idea." She gave her friend a sideways look. "She's the one who told us that Rowan's trees would awaken when confronted with injustice, and cutting them down to build a golf course sounded unjust enough to us!"

Minerva gave them her sly look. "However, to be sure, we decided that we would give them a little push. We used basswood juice to paint our faces green, and then we dressed up as trees by gluing branches and leaves to our clothes using a special paste made from resin. It's a recipe from Morgana — the little girl who wrote the message in the bottle," she told Agatha.

Then she added, "In order to look taller, we climbed on each other's backs." She picked up a funnel-like object from the ground. "I made this using bark." She brought it to her mouth, and her voice came out sounding powerful and thunderously deep. "We are Rowan's trees!"

The mayor clapped his hand. "You did great! That's very ingenious!"

For the first time, Minerva looked uncertain. "In your opinion . . . um . . . did the trees move for real? We couldn't see them, because they were behind us. But I had the feeling that . . . they were kind of following us."

Mutterings rose among the kids. They all had thought they had heard the trees marching onward behind them, but no one had dared look.

The mayor raised a hand to command silence and looked straight into Minerva's hopeful eyes. "The trees followed you," he said. "They walked for real."

Agatha nodded. "I saw them too."

Minerva shifted her gaze from one to the other, trying to understand if they were telling the truth. She felt her toes tingle, but surely that could have been caused by all the dancing she had done. And after all, what did it matter? She believed that in that magic moment between night and day, when everything is possible, the forest had followed them, and so it had to be.

"You set a great example today, children," said the mayor. "The people of Honey Combe have seen an ancient legend come true. And since we are a superstitious people here in Cornwall, they will rise against other injustices and pay less attention to their own interests.

Kitty, who was covered in so many leaves that she looked like a little bush, exclaimed, "Hooray! Who wants a huge stack of chestnut fritters to celebrate?"

The night's activity and emotions had made all the children very hungry, and they welcomed the offer with great enthusiasm.

"We have to go," Agatha said to Minerva. "I met Mrs. Flopps on my way here. She was on her way back to Pembrose in Bert's van."

Thomasina hit her forehead. "Oh no! My parents are coming back from Scotland this morning. If I'm not home by lunchtime, they'll find out!"

"Won't you at least stay for breakfast?" asked a disappointed Alex.

Minerva looked at her new friends, and her heart sank. The corners of her mouth turned down with sadness.

Conrad stepped closer to her. "You're coming back soon to see us, aren't you?"

She looked at his funny ears and his kind eyes. "Of course," she replied. "Are you always going to protect the trees?"

"Always," he answered in a solemn tone.

They shook hands, and Minerva felt that she had found a strong and loyal friend — one she could always rely on.

Anastasia, Jacob, Alex, and Kitty stepped forward to salute the honorary members of Rowan's gang.

The young, tawny-haired fox took off her beautiful green ribbon and gave it to Thomasina. "This way you won't forget me . . ."

"Oh, I couldn't even if I wanted to!" the girl snorted. "You're simply awful."

And to fully express how much she disliked her, she hugged her.

A sneeze interrupted that solemn moment. "*TCHEE-OOO!*" The leaves of a tree shook, and the chough appeared in the middle of the clearing.

"Hey, where have you been the whole time?" Ravi cried.

The little black bird began to fly around Minerva, and then landed on a branch of the old oak tree, which had calmly witnessed the recent events.

Intrigued, the girl followed the bird and climbed up to the branch.

Then she sat astride the branch and asked the little bird, "Are you trying to tell me something?" That's when she noticed the crack in the tree trunk. She put her hand inside it and grabbed the last piece of Morgana's puzzle. The old oak tree had guarded it closely for so many years.

Minerva studied her find and an expression of great wonder appeared on her face. Finally, it all added up.

"Hurry up, Minerva. We have to go!" Agatha called to her.

"I'll be there in a minute!" the girl replied. She laid her hand on the wrinkled, time-marked trunk. "Thank you," she whispered to the old tree and left with her treasure.

CHAPTER 10

MORGANA'S STORY

Agatha's pickup truck was slowly plodding along the curvy country roads.

"Could you go a little faster?" asked Thomasina from the backseat. "If my parents find out that I left without their permission, I'll have to say goodbye to adventures forever."

"I'm going as fast as I can go," Agatha replied a moment before being forced to stop by a sheep that was lying in the middle of the road.

"What a lazy sheep!" Ravi snorted, making a funny face in the rearview mirror.

"Speaking of sheep," Agatha said as they waited for the animal to finish its nap, "you might want to know that a shepherd found old Jim's raft and brought it back to him last night. I ran into him this morning at dawn, and he told me all about it. He was very concerned about you, but I calmed him down saying that I was coming after you."

"Was the raft okay?" asked Ravi.

"Yes," Agatha replied, starting the truck as the sheep's attention had been caught by a tuft of grass on the edge of the road. "Why are you so quiet, Minerva?"

Sitting next to Agatha, the girl was holding something in her lap. The object was absorbing all her attention, so much so, that she wasn't in the least aware of the beautiful scenery that flowed past the truck windows.

Worried about Thomasina's parents, her friends hadn't even noticed what it was that she was holding.

Minerva looked up. "I found this inside a crack in the old oak tree," she said, showing them a diary with the cover made from pressed flowers. "It belonged to Morgana," she added, pointing at the name written with tiny colored pebbles. "It tells what happened to her." She turned to Agatha. "You were right: trees do know humans' every secret. It was a tree that told us Morgana's story."

Then she turned to her friends who, though held back by the seat belts, had craned over to look at the diary. "She's Althea's daughter," she said.

Ravi and Thomasina were speechless.

"It's all written here," Minerva caressed the flower cover. "Morgana was raised by foster parents who couldn't have children," she said. "Good-hearted people with humble origins who lived in the village of Honey Combe. Althea was certain that her daughter would be safe with them, away from the Ravagers of the Sea. She left her an amulet to protect herself and a clue to find the treasure that she had stolen from Black Bart. Unfortunately, though, her foster parents were very possessive and kept any tie to her past away from her, including the truth about her mother.

Then when Morgana was just ten years old, they died, leaving her alone and helpless. She didn't have any other relatives that could take care of her. But her foster parents had written her a letter, where they revealed a little bit of information about her past — including the fact that Althea was her real mother and that she had been part of the Ravagers. And they gave her back her amulet." Minerva held the little flute between her fingers and stopped talking.

"Does that mean that Morgana was the one who hid it in the wall at Lizard Manor?" chimed in a surprised Ravi.

Minerva shook her head. "I don't know," she replied. But she was happy that Morgana had found her mother's amulet: it must have given her some comfort.

She turned to her friends again. "In the letter, they didn't mention the clue to find the Ravagers' treasure. They didn't want to put her life in jeopardy, because they feared that the pirates would have gone after her if they had known that she was alive and that she was looking for the treasure. She would have to beware of them forever. After the death of her foster parents, Morgana felt so hopeless and lonely that she wrote her call for help — the one that we found — and she threw it in the river. Alone, she wandered about in Rowan Forest until she found the old oak tree. She lived there until she was thirteen, hiding from the evil Ravagers."

"That means that the things we saw belonged to her?" asked Thomasina.

"She left them there to tell her story," Minerva explained. "And to help those who, just like her, might have wound up alone in the forest."

"The baby dress was hers then . . ."

"And the lock of hair was Althea's, her mother . . ."

"She drew the map and wrote the recipes for the glue and the sleeping potion . . ."

"What on earth are you talking about?" said Agatha. The story amazed her so much that she could hardly keep her eyes on the road.

Minerva exchanged a look with her friends, who

nodded, giving her their permission to talk. It was okay. They had known Agatha for a long time now, and the witch from the heath moor had helped them every time they had needed her.

"It's a long story," the red-curled girl began. She told her about the Ravagers of the Seas, which Althea was part of. She told her about terrible Black Bart's vengeful jealousy, which had cost Althea her life, and how she had managed to save her daughter, Morgana.

However, she didn't tell her about the Order of the Owls and what they had found out about the people who had lived in Lizard Manor: that was their secret.

"What do you think happened to her?" she finally asked Agatha. "The entries in her diary suddenly stop when she turns thirteen. The rest of her life is missing."

"We don't even know if she found the treasure," Thomasina said.

"And whether or not she managed to escape the Ravagers of the Sea," added Ravi.

Agatha concentrated on the road with a thought-ful look on her face. "I imagine that you'll find out one day," she said with a little smile. "I've known you long enough to know that you won't give up until you find the truth."

Something clattered against Ravi's window.

"Hey, look who's here!" cried the boy. He rolled down the window, and the others also saw the chough flying along next to the pickup truck. Flapping its black wings, it soared and headed for the ocean, which was visible in the distance.

Ravi leaned his black-haired head out of the win-dow and followed it with his eyes. From up there, he could probably dominate the whole Cornish penin-sula with one single look. "I wonder if that really is King Arthur," he said with a sigh.

"I saw the bird the day you found the bottle," Agatha recalled. "I know the legend too. The one about Arthur turning into a chough."

"He's been our guide from the start," Minerva said. "Perhaps that's really him." She smiled. "Perhaps he wanted to make up for the spell cast by Merlin by doing a favor for the people of Honey Combe."

That thought made Ravi happy. He waved his hand out of the window. "So long, Arthur!" he cried at the black bird, which was flying faster than the clouds. "Don't forget you still have to make me a Knight of the Round Table!"

* * *

The day had not yet run out of surprises. In fact, when the kids went back to get their bikes by the edge of the river where they had left them, they found out that someone had left an envelope addressed to Minerva inside the basket of her red bike. There was a message inside:

> *Everybody looks for the place where I hide,*
> *my real identity not a man can provide.*
> *You can't see me, you can't read me.*
> *I'm the Dragon, and you won't catch me.*

They looked around, but the countryside was deserted.

The three children reached the village. As usual, the narrow alleys were full of fishermen, old ladies, and homemakers. Who among them was the Dragon?

"He knows we're looking for him," Ravi whispered.

"And he's challenged us again," muttered Thomasina.

"Well, one thing is certain — he won't scare us!" said Minerva defiantly.

Now, however, someone was coming their way — someone much scarier than the Dragon. Mrs. Orazia Haddok was walking toward them with a watering can in her hands. "Where have you been?" she blurted. "You promised to take care of my garden!"

"Oh, we're so sorry," said Minerva, rushing up to Mrs. Haddok to take the watering can. "We'll do it right now!"

"Unfortunately, I can't stay . . ." Thomasina said in a regretful tone. "Have fun!"

"You're leaving now that we have work to do," muttered an envious Ravi.

Thomasina bent down to give him a kiss on the cheek. "I'll see you soon my valiant Knight of the Hare!" she whispered and then ran away in a whirlpool of curls.

Ravi stood there staring at her, dumbfounded, then he joined Minerva, who was already watering Mrs. Haddok's little garden flowers. Together, they

turned over some earth to make more room between the little plants and finally dropped new seeds in the furrows. They had learned a lot since they had thought gardening was boring.

"Do you think flowers can walk too?" asked Ravi as he looked over the fruits of their labor.

"Well, try not watering them tomorrow, and you'll find out that they'll come to the post office in the middle of the night to give you a piece of their mind!" Minerva replied.

The two friends burst into laughter. Minerva was feeling especially happy. She wasn't afraid of the Dragon and of what the future had in store for them. She had made new friends. The chough was flying in the sky. She was wearing Morgana's lucky charm around her neck. The presence of Althea, the lady of the owls, was felt in the purple heather that grew lushly all around their hideout in the heath moor. The good forces that supported them were plentiful.

At last, Minerva was certain, they would win.

ELISA PURICELLI GUERRA

Elisa at age 3

As a child, I had red hair. It was so red that it led to several nicknames, the prettiest of which was Carrot. With my red hair, I wanted to be Pippi Longstocking for two reasons. The first reason was that I wanted to have the strength to lift a horse and show him to everyone! The second was that every night my mother read Astrid Lindgren's books to me until she nearly lost her voice (or until I graciously allowed her to go to bed). As I fell asleep each night, I hoped to wake up at Villa Villacolle. Instead, I found myself in Milan. What a great disappointment!

After all of Lindgren's books were read and reread, my mother, with the excuse that I was grown up, refused to continue to read them again. So I began to tell stories myself. They were serialized stories, each more and more intricate than the one before and chock-full of interesting characters. Pity then, the next morning, when I would always forget everything.

Elisa today

At that point I had no choice; I started to read myself. I still remember the book that I chose: a giant-sized edition of the Brothers Grimm fairy tales with a blue cloth cover.

Today my hair is less red, but reading is still my favorite pastime. Pity it is not a profession because it would be perfect for me!

GABO LEÓN BERNSTEIN

I was born in Buenos Aires, Argentina, and have had to overcome many obstacles to become an illustrator.

"You cannot draw there," my mom said to me, pointing to the wall that was smeared.

"You cannot draw there," the teacher said to me, pointing to the school book that was messed.

"Draw where you want to . . . but you were supposed to hand over the pictures last week," my publishers say to me, pointing to the calendar.

Currently I illustrate children's books, and I'm interested in video games and animation projects. The more I try to learn to play the violin, the more I am convinced that illustrating is my life and my passion. My cat and the neighbors rejoice in it.

Gabo

FIND OUT
MORE ABOU
MINERV,
MINT
AND HER
FRIENDS AT
WWW.CAPSTONEKIDS.CO